Written by Dana Meachen Rau
Illustrated by Jane Conteh-Morgan

Reading Advisers:

Gail Saunders-Smith, Ph.D., Reading Specialist

Dr. Linda D. Labbo, Department of Reading Education,
College of Education, The University of Georgia

LEVEL A

Ⓐ

A COMPASS POINT
EARLY READER

For Dad

A Note to Parents

As you share this book with your child, you are showing your new reader what reading looks like and sounds like. You can read to your child anywhere—in a special area in your home, at the library, on the bus, or in the car. Your child will associate reading with the pleasure of being with you.

This book will introduce your young reader to many of the basic concepts, skills, and vocabulary necessary for successful reading. Talk through the details in each picture before you read. Then read the book to your child. As you read, point to each word, stopping to talk about what the words mean and the pictures show. Your child will begin to link the sounds of the letters with the look of the words that you and he or she read.

After your child is familiar with the story, let him or her read the story alone. Be careful to let the young reader make mistakes and correct them on his or her own. Be sure to praise the young reader's abilities. And, above all, have fun.

Gail Saunders-Smith, Ph.D.
Reading Specialist

Compass Point Books
3722 West 50th Street, #115
Minneapolis, MN 55410

Visit Compass Point Books on the Internet at *www.compasspointbooks.com* or e-mail your request to *custserv@compasspointbooks.com*

Library of Congress Cataloging-in-Publication Data

Rau, Dana Meachen, 1971–
    Ways to go / by Dana Meachen Rau ; illustrated by J. Conteh-Morgan.
        p. cm.
    ISBN 0-7565-0071-0
        1. Transportation—Juvenile literature. [1. Transportation.] I. Conteh-Morgan, Jane ill. II. Title.
    HE152 .R38 2001
    388—dc21   00-011843

Car. Truck.

Plane.

Balloon.

Lots of ways to go.

Bike.

Horse.

Bus.

Wheelchair.

Sledding in the
snow.

Boat.

Train.

Skates.

Wagon.

Walking
with two feet.

My favorite way
from here to there

**is skipping
down the street!**